SIR

THE VOYAGE

PARTH AGARWAL

I dedicate this book to my spirit of imagination

Contents

Foreword

This book is going to develop a lot of respect for Sir. It makes a reader feel the powers Sir uses. Sir lies on the thin line of good and evil and different readers would interpret this characater differently. This book takes one on a ride of variety of thoughts.

Preface

This story explores developement of Sir as a strong character physically as well as mentally. This story also extends the broders where PSU's stories take place. It also setups characters that may turn out to be very important in the future.

Acknowledgements

I would like to thank my family for providing me an independent environment where I could allow my imagination to take flight.

CHAPTER ONE

STARTING A JOURNEY

The threat of Kaal was over. Sir had nothing to do. Shield and its agencies scanned for any fishy activities. If found, ASF would start working on it.

Sir went back to Tins on Shield's new spacecraft. Sir explored Tins. He came to know that Shield Lord was not present there and the planet was administered by his ministers. Sir did not think much and went to a open field. A herd of seven horses grabbed his attention. They were racing against each other. Soon they flew up in the air. A stableboy threw a leash at one of the horses and pulled it. The others followed the horse. Sir, interested to know about the horses, went and inquired about the horses. The boy greeted Sir and said, " These horses are siblings. Their father was a royal horse who served the king and had magical powers. He was looked after my grandfather. In a war, the father got heavily injured and was discharged from royal services. Due to their affection for the horse, my grandfather left the royal stable. He built a small stable here." Sir felt bad for the boy's grandfather. He asked the boy for the horses and in return, Sir would give him a job at the royal stable. The boy got confused. He ran and called his father. His father did not want the horses to return to a royal descendent but due to the severe need for money, he had to agree to the deal.

Sir sat on the eldest horse and rode it to the castle. He got a chariot attached to those horses. The horses could travel through far distances even in space. Sir stood on the chariot and went to explore different planets.

CHAPTER TWO

BORN OF RUDRA

Sir travelled to the first planet: Orsnol

Sir landed on this planet. He could see giants everywhere. The planet had a high temperature. Sir could see elephants pulling carts filled with some metal scrap. He followed one of the carts that led to a factory. Lava was transported to machines there through pipes having their source in a lake. He saw Giants hammering metals. He soon realised it was a weapon factory. He sneaked into the factory and saw the process. The metal scraps were reacted with different chemicals to form metal. The metal was then put into a large furnace powered by Lava. The melted metals were then shaped into different shapes and handles were attached to them for opertaing. The shaped weapons were then carried to a room covered with curtains. He peeped inside. He saw four wizards reading and encrypting some spells on the weapons.

Sir was observing them when a Giant picked him up. He took him to a man wearing a crown. He seemed like the king of the planet. The king tried to talk to Sir but Sir showed his arrogance. So the King ordered Sir to be punished. Sir was taken to Colosseum Arena. He had to fight with two Giants. One carried a Flail and the other carried a Mace. They both came to fight with Sir. Sir summoned Sword Of Tins from the sky. The force by which it hit Sir's hand made the Giant fall. Sir was going to attack a Giant with the sword when a wizard held Sir's hand. The wizard begged not to use the sword. Sir agreed on one condition, He wanted to complete the fight with an ordinary sword. The wizard took the Sword of Tins and handed him an ordinary sword. The Giants attacked Sir. Sir ran between one of the Giant's legs. Sir put a cut into his leg. The other giant hit Sir with his Flail. Sir held the flail and pulled the Giant towards him. Sir punched his face. Sir and the two giants had a good fight. Sir also faced some injuries. Soon Sir defeated both of them. The king came down to attend to Sir and took him to the palace. Sir was given a seat. The King asked Sir how he got the Sword of Tins. Sirtold him the whole story. The King told Sir about Orsnol. Orsnol was a planet that specialised in making weapons. All kinds of weapons were made here and the sword of Tins was also made and enchanted there. The king was the first to start making weapons on the planet. He used a metal found only in Orsnol called the Asht. The king gave back the Sword of Tins to Sir. He also gifted Sir a golden chariot for the seven horses instead of a wooden one. He gave Sir a war outfit consisting of a sash made of the skin of a lion, a dhoti, a cape, and a war crown. He also gave Sir many weapons like Trident, battle axe, bow, swords, shield and arrows with different powers.

This form of Sir riding a seven-horsed golden chariot loaded with different weapons and a war horn wearing a war outfit was named Rudra.

Sir flew in his chariot over the Lava lake and left Orsnol.

CHAPTER THREE

MENTAL STRENGTH

Sir entered a new planet called Taxila. Taxila was a very small flat planet. It was resided by seven very intelligent saints. The planet was guarded by different armies provided by kings in exchange for teachings. The soldiers stopped Sir from reaching the seven saints. Sir defeated the soldiers. He reached the seven saints. He tried to attack them but they captured Sir with their spells. Sir was put into a cage. When the seven saints were gone, he broke free and started to attack the saints individually. He did not harm any of the saints. He captured them. He asked them about themselves.

The seven saints held all the knowledge. They knew every spell that had ever existed. They wrote the spells which gave powers to many people. Sir asked them to help him. He wanted to gain knowledge from them. The seven saints saw potential in Sir to hold the knowledge they have. They did not teach Sir everything they knew because that would make him undefeatable and immortal which would be against the laws of nature. Sir took months of training from them. He learnt to manipulate fire, and create a shield around him. He did not need to carry weapons physically with him now. He could summon his weapon with spells. Sir could now summon a dangerous snake whenever he wished. With a spell, Sir now could increase his number of hands.

Sir learned more about the saints. He came to know that the saints had written the books from which Shastri Ji and his companions gained powers.

Sir wanted to take the saints with him. The saints agreed to stay with Sir but they did not wish to travel from planet to planet. So the saints promised to stay with him when his voyage was over.

Sir left Taxila on a mission to win over Tin's solar system having over thirty planets.

CHAPTER FOUR

ONE VERSUS THE ARMY

After Taxila Sir travelled to Kuruk. He found out there that the place was hit by a box called the Divine box. It gave powers to 25 good people called the divinities. Sir also wanted to capture them. Sir went to their meeting place. There were only 5 superheroes. Sir asked them to come with him. They declined. Sir threatened them. They started to attack Sir. Sir summoned a crescent shaped sword. He went up to his chariot and moved toward the heroes.

One of them turned invisible and spawned behind Sir. He pushed Sir down. Sir fell. He summoned his bow and hit an arrow at the divinity who was turning invisible. He fainted. Sir rode his chariot back and picked his sword up. Another divinity threw a fire ball toward him. Sir also defended with a fireball. Sir jumped and landed near the 4 left. He fought them with his sword and shield. While he was fighting, other divinities reached there. Sir was surrounded with them. A divinity who could run very fast punched him. Sir created a shield dome around him. It trapped the fast-running divinity. He beat the divinity with a mace to unconsciousness. He summoned 10 arms and lifted the shield dome. A divinity caught Sir's hand with his hair. Sir pulled her and pierced him with his sword. Sir then with his battle axe ran through the army of divinities. He killed many of them. Then he put three arrows in his bow and shot them. He was left with just 5 divinities. He summoned a deadly snake and one of the most powerful weapons: his special trident. He fought the 5 together. The snake killed the two and Sir killed two with both sides of his trident. He was just left with a divinity that had healing power.

Sir's snake caught him. Sir forced him to heal everybody. All the divinities were healed but were unconscious. He buried everybody with the divine box except divinities with abilities of fire named Agni, ice named Himvat, wind named Vayu, land named budh, electricity named Indar, and healing named Sushrut. Sir asked them to join him and the divinities being impressed by his powers, agreed.

CHAPTER FIVE

FIGHT BETWEEN KINGS

Sir now had five superheroes to make commanders of his army. Sir took Sushrut with him in his chariot, untied five horses from his chariot, and gave one to each of the other superheroes. They flew out of Kuruk.

They entered a place called Ayedha. The planet was beautiful. There was greenery. Buildings had gold symbols on them. People wore long cloth tied around their bodies.

Sir inquired about the kingdom from one of the residents, he gave Sir details about the king and also mentioned that he had recently lost one of his sons named Zordian who died on Earth. Sir understood that it was the same Zordian who was helping Fan. Sir moved further. There were soldiers wearing golden armor. They held spears and rode horses. On seeing them enter two of the guards caught them and asked to come with them to the castle. But Sir and the divinities refused to go with them as vulnerable. Before they could attack, Himvat froze them. budh created a hole and put the soldiers in it.

Sir sent Agni to the castle to warn the king. Sir needed control over this planet and also soldiers for his army. The

Golden Gladiator refused and insulted Agni. Agni with a fireball broke the king's throne. The king ordered the guards to kill Agni. The Guards tried to catch him but Agni burnt them alive. He whistled. One of the horses arrived and took Agni to Sir. Soon they came to hear the news that the King was planning to attack them. Sir prepared himself and the divinities. The next day, Sir saw an army of roughly 5000 soldiers march towards them. Sir took his battle axe in hand and ran towards the army. He rammed through the shields of the soldiers. Soon the army started getting reduced. It all came to the army chief. He was sitting on his elephant. Sir jumped and pushed the elephant, making it fall. The army chief got up. Sir cast a spell and his axe disappeared and his sword and shield appeared. He, holding his weapon, struck a blow on the chief's shoulder pads. Sir saved himself from the chief with a shield. Sir read a spell again. The sword started to shine. Sir quickly pierced the sword through the chief's abdomen. On piercing, the sword created flames around it and the chief burnt to death.

Sir returned to where the divinities and he was staying. The news of the defeat reached the king. He was astonished. He understood it was not going to be an easy war. King alarmed all his army to prepare for a war. The army prepared all night. At dawn, a soldier on a horse placed notice all over the kingdom. The notice said all people to stay inside their houses. The king wore his golden gladiator outfit. He rode a chariot with a charioteer. The army consisted of over ten thousand infantry soldiers, five thousand archers and artillery. The army was headed by the King, the Queen also known as the Mark Archer, the Prince also known as the Golden Prince, The Princess named Tara, and a few army officers. The army marched towards Sir and his team with war horns. Sir heard the sound and asked the divinities to get ready for war. Sir read a spell to cover him and his team with armor. Sir turned from his normal form to his Rudra form. He got on his chariot. The divinities 1also got on their horses. Sir's four more hands appeared. He held shield in one hand, battle axe in one, trident in one, sword in one, and bow and arrow in the rest. Agni and Himvat stood in front. Sir followed them. At the back stood budh, Vayu, and Indar. Sushrut was left behind at the house. The six marched towards the army. Sir blew the war horn and the war started. Sir ran his chariot towards the king.

The sky turned dark. Everybody was scared of seeing the ultimate Rudra form. The infantry was handled by budh and Indar. Agni and Vayu handled the archers. Himvat froze down the artillery. budh created a hole and buried a large number of soldiers. Indar launched lightning blasts on the soldiers. Sir was engaged by and stopped by some soldiers. Sir jumped off the chariot and just by the effect of his landing, the soldiers fell. The chariot returned to bring Sushrut. Sir was killing tens of soldiers together. Sushrut got on the chariot. The royal (king, queen, prince, and princess) surrounded the chariot carrying Sushrut. They started fighting with Sushrut. Sushrut lacked fighting skills but still gave a tough fight to the royals. He fought till his last breath. The news of Sushrut being killed reached Sir. Sir killed every soldier in his surroundings and flew. He landed in the heart of the Royals. Army Officers also arrived there. Sir was standing in the centre of a circle formed by people aiming to kill him. Sir started fighting with his six hands. The royals and officers were putting in all of their efforts. The ten army officers were killed with bows and arrows. All that was left were the royals.

The King attacked Sir. Sir dodged his attack. Sir made his hands disappear. He fought the Golden Gladiator with sword and shield. The King continuously attacked Sir. Sir defended himself with the shield. The Mark archer saw the divinities coming towards them. So, the prince, the princess, and the queen tackled the divinities. On the other hand, Sir had defended many blows. It was now time to attack. Sir pushed the king with his shield. The king hit a wall and fell. Sir bought himself a bow and arrow with the spells. Sir loaded two arrows into the bow and shot them in a way that both of the king's hands were pierced with an arrow each. Sir read a spell and glowing chains appeared around the king's wrists and feet. The king rose up in the air. The king was stuck up in the air. Sir decided not to kill him. Sir left the king to suffer. Sir also made the prince rise up high in the air. The prince went higher and higher. Soon he was out of sight and then suddenly he fell from a great height. The prince died. The divinities by then had already defeated the rest of the royals and Himvat had put them in a chamber of ice.

Sir freed the queen and the princess. Sir was impressed by the princess and her qualities. Sir asked her to accompany him. Princess Tara was confused, because Sir was the new ruler of Ayedha but was also the killer of her two brothers. On seeing the humbleness of Sir, she agreed to accompany him. The queen inquired what Sir would do to the King. Sir said in a time span of 20 days with no food and water, the king's only wish would be death. When the king would want relief from the torture, Sir would heal him and then offer him to join Sir on his voyage. Sir stayed there for twenty days. Sir in those twenty days conducted a big spell which lasted for five days to absorb the powers of Sushrut. Sir interacted with the public and took a tour of the kingdom.

Sir before leaving asked the Queen to be his representative in Ayedha and rule the place under his orders. Sir also asked Tara and the king to stay there till his voyage was over. While leaving, Sir saw the king's charioteer. Sir was very impressed by him in the war. Sir asked him to become his charioteer. The charioteer agreed. Sir healed him and took him with himself. While interacting with him, Sir came to know that his name was Kha. Kha was very well educated. He knew a lot about travelling. He told Sir that on seeing the seven horses, he knew that they were destined to lose. Kha mentioned that a folk tale mentioned about seven horses that looked the same as Sir's. Sir was happy and a little surprised to know this.

A new chariot was brought by Vayu and Indar from Orsnol. Sir stood behind and Kha sat in front.

ARE THEY IN HELL?

Sir reached a planet full of skeletons. It was the planet from which Deadhead belonged. The planet was covered with white sand and the planet was under a permanent solar eclipse. The king of the planet was the father of Deadhead. He saw Sir. He invited him for dinner. Sir agreed. At the dinner table, Sir mentioned his plan to conquer the planets he visited and also about how he defeated Kaal on Earth. After everyone had their meal. The Skeleton king flipped the table and picked his weapon (a hammer with spikes on it) to attack Sir. Sir started to read a spell and before he could complete it, the king hit him. Sir went through a wall, creating a hole in it. Himvat created a thick wall of ice but the king broke it. The king threw the hammer in such a way that all the divinities fell down. The weapon was then hit and stuck on the wall. It created a crack in it. Sir threw a spear at the king. The king picked it up and put a cut on Kha's hand. Sir now knew that the king was strong. Sir made a staff appear in his hand. He hit the staff on the king's head. The king fell. The king came out of the building. The king started to attack Sir. He missed him again and again. His missed shots landed on the walls of the building they were having their meal in. After a few shots, the building collapsed. The collapsing building was going to hit the divinities but budh created a shield of hardened sand around them and Kha. All of them were saved. The king raised one of his hands in the air and then hit the ground with it. Skeletons started coming out of the land and skeleton warriors wearing armor started coming toward them. Agni burnt the skeletons, Vayu hit the skeleton with high winds which caused them to dismantle. Vayu froze them and then budh crushed them. Indar fell lightning on the skeletons. All the divinities were fighting. Kha was sitting and healing himself on the chariot.

Sir brought himself his strongest sword but the sword did no effect on the king. So, he brought himself a mace and started smashing the king. The king counter-attacked. Sir after many tries weakened him. Soon after the skeletons were not spawning. The divinities came together and killed the king for Sir. Sir then picked up the king's skull and attached it to his staff.

Kha came and said that he had read about that planet. The planet had a place that could open a portal that was never crossed by anyone. They all started searching for the place. budh found a metal table coming out of the land. It had a hole to place something. Others came to budh. Sir started reading inscriptions written on it. The table said that a dead body was to be placed there to open a portal. Sir had learned to create life from the saints. He with all his powers created a kid. He had no option but to kill that kid. The kid's body was placed on the table. A portal opened. Sir was unable to walk. He dragged himself onto the chariot and ordered Kha to take the chariot through it. The chariot was unable to go through the portal. Kha thought of uniting the seven horses and then trying. No other person could have crossed this portal because for that one had to escape the skeletons, then sacrifice a life, and then cross that portal with a very fast and powerful vehicle. The seven horses were united. The divinities stood beside Sir on the chariot and then went through the portal.

CHAPTER SEVEN

OUT OF HELL?

The new place was scarier than the last planet. There was darkness. Sir and the divinities started to lose their lives there. It was hell, the place where death resided. The divinities went unconscious and then lost their breath. Kha remained alive with his power to heal. He saw Sir fainting. He sacrificed his life and with all his powers healed Sir to life and himself died. Sir now was in full power. He was no longer affected by the effects of hell. Sir stood up. He was shocked on realising that he was standing in front of Death. Sir was afraid for the first time. Death took out his staff by which he could take anybody's soul out of the body. Sir escaped from the staff. Sir ran towards death and pushed the staff off his hand. Death took out his mace and a noose. He caught Sir with the noose, pulled Sir towards himself, and hit him with a mace. He hanged Sir on a platform. Sir with a spell saved himself from getting suffocated with the rope. Death continuously hit Sir with mace. Sir started to bleed. He could only move his hands. Sir wished to die just to get relief from this torture. Death hit Sir's head with the mace. Sir died.

Death revived him and started to beat him again. Before Sir could reach the point of wanting to die, he burnt the rope with a spell and fell down. He picked up his trident and hit Death with it but nothing happened to him. Death hit Sir and Sir went high up in the sky and then fell. Sir took out his strongest arrow of which he had only one. He hit Death with it. Death fell but nothing happened to him. Sir understood that the spells and weapons would not work on Death as he is above all. Sir instead of killing him, took out a wheel that was full of arrows. The wheel was huge. It covered the sky and arrows started flying out of it. All of Death's workers started to die. Hell was destroyed. The sky started to clear. Death feared that hell would fall apart. He joined his hands and requested to take back the weapon. Sir agreed on one condition that Death would give all his powers to Sir. For Death, his responsibilities came before himself. Death gave all his powers to Sir. Sir took back his wheel. Sir took out his sword. Sir put the sword in Death's head and left it there. Sir did not realise that now, he had to carry out the responsibilities of Death. He could not leave Hell and was now obliged to maintain it. Sir again made Hell how it was. Sir revived his team. He asked Kha and Agni to bring a giant from Orsnol and the seven saints. For a week Sir carried out Death's responsibilities. After a week, the seven saints made him immune to the staff and the giant made a staff with the same powers. Sir erased the giant's memory so that he could not make any more staff. Sir revived the king of the skeletons and made him the king of hell. The king remained thankful to Sir. Sir and his team moved out from the portal. Sir revived the kid they had killed. Sir adopted him as his son and named him Omkaar. Everyone moved from the planet. They all reached a barren planet.

CHAPTER EIGHT

IS THIS THE END?

Sir and his team reached a barren planet resided only by an owl. Sir decided to make his castle on that planet.

Sir named the barren planet Kailash. He read spells along with the seven saints and a beautiful and large castle was created. The seven saints performed some rituals on the planet for the betterment of Sir. After the rituals were over, bad energy got erased. The barren planet became fertile.

When the seven saints and Sir were getting up after the rituals they entered a spiritual world. They saw the planet they were standing on, talking. The planet thanked them for the rituals. The planet was earlier resided by a great king but later, it was occupied by and exploited by a tribe of demons belonging to another solar system called Daino. Daino at some point used to trouble the planets in Sir's Solar System. Sir ignored the topic. The planet continued with the topic. The planet mentioned that it had once been so powerful that it could move at the pace and in the direction that the ruler wished and desired. Sir was happy to know that. The saints and Sir woke up and came back from the spiritual world.

Shield Lord arrived in Kailash to meet Sir. Sir asked where Shield Lord was but Shield Lord ignored his words.. Shield Lord met the Seven Saints. The Saints sensed pureness in Shield Lord. Sir insisted the saints give some teachings to Shield Lord also. After a ten hour long session, Shield Lord was open to a totally new and different world. Shield Lord could now create matter. Shield Lord decided to meditate in his own place. He left Kailash. The Saints also gave some teachings to Tara. Sir wanted her father also to come to Kailash. Golden Gladiator came and begged Sir to bring back his son from hell. Sir said that tampering with the laws of nature again and again would cause disbalance. Prince could only be brought back if anyone close to him sacrifices. The Golden Gladiator insisted on taking his life and bringing back the Prince as the King had lived his life but the Prince was very young. Sir was convinced. Sir touched the Golden Gladiator with his staff of death. The King's soul left the body and the Prince's soul entered the body. Sir read a spell and made the body young. Saints also gave some teachings to the Prince. The Prince was renamed Anish.

Anish's naming ceremony had just completed when a man riding an elephant entered Kailash. The man said that he was sent by the court of Gods and he was there to punish Sir for interfering in the workings of Hell. The man introduced himself. He was Sakar, the King of Swarg, the planet where the court of Gods was placed. He was the greatest known warrior and was undefeated. Sir did not take him seriously. Sir asked the divinities to handle him. The divinities created an arc around him riding his elephant. The divinities advanced to attack him. Sakar pulled out five daggers and threw them towards them. One dagger hit one each. All of them fell on the ground unconscious. Sir understood that Sakar was powerful. Anish hit Sakar with a javelin. Skara pulled the javelin out of himself. Nothing happened to him. Anish took out a mace and started to attack. Sakar took out a noose and caught Anish's mace. Anish pulled the noose, making Sakar fall. Sakar and Anish then got into a sword fight. Sakar broke Anish's sword and kicked him far away. Tara took out a bow and fired an arrow into the sky. The arrow multiplied. The sky was filled with thousands of arrows. Sakar created a dome around him. The dome saved him from the arrows. Sakar then took out his bow and shot an arrow towards Tara. Tara failed to dodge and got hit with the arrow. Tara was unable to move her body. Sakar then shot an arrow at her. The arrow was going to hit Tara when Sir saved her by hitting the arrow with his sword. Sir freed Tara from the effects of the arrow. Sir asked Tara to get back and let him fight. Sir took out his battle axe. Sakar got back on his elephant. Sir jumped high to attack Sakar. Sakar could see Sir's angry face and six hands of which one holded an axe. Sakar aimed a light beam at Sir. Sir dodged the beam with his axe. Sir's axe was going to hit Sakar's neck, Sakar punched Sir's hand. Sir hit and made Sakar's crown fall. Sakar got angry. The Sky got covered with clouds. Sakar looked up in the sky and a light from the clouds came to his chest. His hands got bright. His eyes turned into bright blue light. He started to shoot light beams at Sir with his full potential. Sir was dodging the attacks but one of the beams hit him. Sir fell. Sakar's two more hands and four more head appeared. He got down from the elephant and started to walk towards Sir who had gotten weak. Tara came running towards him to stop him but Sakar pushed her with a beam without even looking at him. The Seven Saints appeared in front of him. He insisted they move. He did not want to harm those who had been passing on the knowledge of ancestors. He made that portion of land on which they were standing float in the air. Sakar jumped on Sir and squeezed his face. He punched him continuously. Sir was bleeding heavily. Kha ran the chariot into Sakar. Sakar fell far away. Sakar's elephant came running towards the chariot but Kha moved the chariot. The seven horses left the chariot and started fighting with the elephant. They continuously hit him by him running towards him and jumping on him. The Elephant got tired and fell. Anish and the Divinities woke up. Tara with them came towards Sakar. Vayu lifted him remotely with air and made him fall into a hole created by Budh, they both buried his lower half. Tara and Anish took out maces and started to hit him. Agni put fire on him. Himvat then froze him. Indar hit him with lightning. Anish and Tara then started to hit him with mace. After some hitting, a light beam again fell on Sakar. Sakar with a blast of light beam made everyone fall far away. He got up and his body healed. He threw a dagger high in the sky. The dagger multiplied to seven and came falling towards Anish, Tara and the Divinities but were stopped by one of the Seven Saints. The other Six Saints healed Sir and gave him new powers. Sir got up. He rode a horse. A green sword made of light appeared in his hand. Snakes revolved around the sword. Sakar came running towards Sir. Agni shot a fireball below Sakar. Sakar flew up and Sir put the sword into Sakar's chest. Sakar fell on the ground. His body got covered with snakes and then his body disappeared. The Elephant was made to return to the court of Gods with a note mentioning what had happened to Sakar. Now, Sir became the king of Swarg and was now the most powerful warrior.

CHAPTER NINE

THE END

After the fight, The Seven Saints went into the meditating form. Their meditation would complete after a year. In that time span, Sir and Tara gave Omkaar many teachings. Omkaar also gained powers but he could use them when he got older. Also, Tara gave birth to a son. The boy was named Kumar. After the meditation of seven saints was over, they gave a boon to Kumar and Omkaar. Both of them grew to the age of twenty in a span of one month and then returned to normal ageing. Kumar developed fighting skills and became the head of the army. Sir asked the saints to design his court. The saints had the members in mind. They asked Sir to wait for two weeks. Two weeks later, Sir's court was ready and Sir wore the crown of the planet and sat on the throne.

Sir on the throne, entered a new form : Kartavir. He had grown a grey beard. He carried a sceptre with him. He wore a dress made of gold with a red cape. Hands of his throne had the face of a roaring lion and an owl sat on the shoulder of Kartavir.

He headed the court of Kailash. His throne was on an elevated platform, ten stairs high. Five stairs down his throne was a platform where Tara's and Shield Lord's thrones were placed. The stairs ended in a circle shaped hall. On the left side of the stairs were thrones of Anish and the Seven saints. On the opposite side were thrones of Omkaar, Kumar, Agni, Indar, Vayu, budh, Himvat and Kha in the respective order. Both sides had one extra throne at the end each for important guests. Between the ends of both sides was the gate for the court. Each of the members was alloted with an assistant. Each one of them were also given their roles. Tara handled the home ministry of Sir's kingdom. Shield Lord was the King Father and was the chief advisor of Sir. Anish made war strategies and Kumar looked after the training of the army. Omkaar was given the duty to look after technological advancements and writing of new spells with the saints. The divinities were given the duty to look after different parts of Sir's kingdom. Kha assisted Sir. On the first day of the court, Shield Lord arrived in Kailash after completing his meditation. Shield Lord taught him a spell which would summon a very special weapon. Shield Lord then said to Sir that he was called to Swarg. Sir was confused as to why was he called and how did Shield Lord know he was called.

Sir planned to talk to him about it later and first focus on his responsibilities as Kartavir. Administration of Sir's kingdom was very well planned. His kingdom continued to flourish.